KU-035-932

NESSIE'S ADVENTURES–No. 1

The Tourists

THE TOURISTS

"Och Nessie, ye cannae go scarin' folk tonight, yiv yer tea tae get an' homework to do," said mum, as she stirred her steaming pot.

Nessie curled herself around a rock — and sulked. Her mum knew it wasn't easy to be a thirty foot long monster and go to school, and do homework, when all young Nessie wanted to do was play.

Nessie and her mum lived in a cave, eight hundred feet down in the middle of Loch Ness. The deepest, darkest part of the loch was where all the monsters lived, as no human beings could ever reach that deep.

Nessie loved the calm summer nights, when the sun glistened through the trees that surrounded the loch. It made them look like sentinels and, often, they mirrored themselves on the still surface of the water.

"It's a perfect night for scaring the folks" she thought to herself and, although she DID look scary, she had a lot to learn.

She quickly ate her evening meal of fresh, still-wriggling salmon, followed by a tasty mixture of freshwater jellied eels and soft juicy snails. She rattled through her homework, which included reading the short story - 'How to Be Scary in the Moonlight,' and left the cave to have some fun.

It was the tourist season now and most of the visitors were here to see 'the monster' — so Nessie didn't want to disappoint them. She started her routine on the surface of the loch, circling round and round, stretching her long neck in the air and arranging her snake-like body into three humps. She widened her circle when she spotted a family of tourists camped on the shore. She saw cameras flash in the distance and heard voices drifting towards her through the calm air.

"Look Mom, it's the monster," the little boy shouted, looking through his binoculars. "It looks like a gigantic black eel with three big humps and a long neck.

Can we chase it in our boat — can we, dad?".
The boy was persistent, and the parents relented.

"Oh,oh - the American tourists are back" Nessie
said to herself, recognising the accent, so she
speeded up her display to excite them even more.

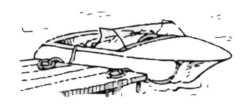

Mom and Dad leapt into a shiny new red and
white speedboat with their little son, revved the
engine to its maximum pitch and, within a minute,
were almost upon Nessie. She loved being chased...
and slowly submerged...... She watched the
underside of the boat pass over her and, when she
surfaced a minute later, she was just in time to see
the boat hit a floating tree stump, shoot up out of
the water, then plummet back down again. The
family of three was thrown into the air and - as if in
slow motion - one by one they landed in the water a
few feet from their sinking boat.

'Typical,' Nessie thought — 'not one life jacket between them'. She had to move quickly and serpentined through the water - firstly to the boy, who was flapping around wildly. She swam underneath him and lifted his small body out of the water, balancing it on her back, which was broad and long. He screamed with excitement. Mom was next. Nessie plucked her from the water using her small sharp teeth, which nobody saw unless she wanted them to, and placed her beside her son. She then swept up the dazed father and slowly zig-zagged towards the edge of the loch, being careful not to lose any of her cargo.

Once Mom realised what was happening, she became hysterical.
"We're going to be eaten," she shrieked, as she clung to the unusually warm but slippery surface.
"It's O.K. Mom" the boy shouted. "The monster is saving us!"

Nessie slowly delivered the three humans safely to the sandy shore, then swam back to the middle of the loch. Raising her head and long neck straight out of the water, she folded her huge body into three humps and swam round and round. The family stared in awe at the black monster silhouetted against the now setting sun. Realising what had just happened, all the family waved and shouted - "Goodbye Nessie… and thank you"…

Nessie nodded her head up and down, as if to acknowledge, and slowly slipped under the water.

"I hope you hivnae been gettin' up tae mischief tonight" said Mum, when Nessie got back to the cave. She worried about her little monster but she couldn't tell Nessie about the special powers she had inherited — the powers which caused her father to be taken from them… no… she would wait a bit longer…

Nessie curled her long body around her favourite rock but, before she fell asleep, she planned her next adventure… tomorrow, she would visit Jess and Tilly, her mermaid friends who lived in the next cave.

NESSIE'S ADVENTURES - No. 2
Jess and Tilly

Jess and Tilly

Nessie awoke, feeling happy. It was Saturday morning and she had no school for a whole two days. As she uncoiled herself from around her rock she heard her mum shout, "Breakfast's ready, Nessie".

After her breakfast of jellied eels and snails she decided to visit her mermaid friends Jess and Tilly, who lived in the next cave. She zig-zagged her long eel-like body through the water and as she neared their cave she heard crying. Inside the cave Jess sat on a rock with her head in her hands and her long, blonde hair cascading over her shaking body. "Jess, what is it, what's wrong?" asked Nessie. "It's Tilly, she's gone. Mum is away visiting our auntie and when I woke up this morning I couldn't find Tilly".

Tilly was Jess's twin sister and never left her side. It was always a beautiful sight to see when they swam together, their tails swaying in

synchronised motion, with their long golden hair trailing behind them.

"Come on, I'll help you look for her" said Nessie, and they swam out of the cave into the deep, dark water.

They tried all the caves in the area - with no luck - then they met Terry Trout. Terry had a big, ugly face with sharp teeth which hung outside his fat, bottom lip, making him look frightening, but he was as gentle as a pussycat. Everybody liked Terry Trout and they tried not to laugh when he spoke.

"I faw Tilly earlier wif Quiddy", he said, spitting as he spoke, "they were heading for the middle of the loch. Quiddy wof holding Tilly in hif long armf…".

"Thanks", said Nessie - as she and Tilly quickly swam off.

Nessie had a bad feeling in her stomach. Squiddy was a giant, forty-three foot long squid with eight long arms, which could crush you to death in an instant, and the rumours were that, if he squirted his dark blue inky liquid on you, you could die. He also had an attitude. Nobody liked Squiddy — and

Squiddy liked nobody!

The centre of the loch was the deepest part, where no one ever ventured. It was unusual for a giant squid to be in a loch — but who was going to question a creature of such a size? Nessie and Jess swam to the surface of the water, opened their mouths and filled their bodies with air, before plunging down into the deep water again.

When they arrived at Squiddy's cave they slowly swam through the entrance in silence. They had to be careful because Squiddy could change colour to the same as his surroundings so you wouldn't see him until he moved. A large cage came into view and -curled up asleep at the bottom of the cage - was Tilly the mermaid. Jess swam up to the cage and whispered..

"Tilly - wake up. Tilly - wake up".

With heavy eyelids, Tilly opened her big blue eyes. "Where am I?" she asked, with a croaky voice. She didn't know it but Squiddy had seen Tilly swimming around the entrance to her home cave and decided to kidnap her. He squirted his inky liquid around her and when she swallowed it, she fell fast asleep.

There was a huge padlock on the cage door. With both hands, Jess tried pulling, but it wouldn't budge.

"Stand back" Nessie said. She put her face up close to the cage and stared at the huge padlock. And she stared… and she stared…

Jess couldn't be sure but she thought she saw a beam of yellow light flowing from Nessie's eyes to the padlock. All of a sudden, the lock turned white and fell to pieces - right before her very eyes. Jess swung open the cage door and swam inside. She put her arm round Tilly's waist.
"Hold on to me, Tilly"….and they both swam out of the cage.

Nessie, Tilly and Jess headed for the entrance to the cave and, just as it came into view, a darkness fell over them. They stopped swimming and floated quietly, looking around them. The entrance was blocked… by Squiddy! He was much bigger than Nessie, with long tentacles waving around in all directions. His huge, bulging eyes darted here and there and his gigantic mouth, opening wide, was ready to swallow up his three visitors. "Get behind me," said Nessie to the girls - and the mermaids swam to the end of Nessie's thirty foot body.

"Hold on to my tail", she said, as she focused her eyes in the centre of Squiddy's massive body, which covered the whole cave entrance. She stared, and she stared... and she stared... All of a sudden a huge hole appeared in the middle of Squiddy's body. Nessie could see the outside of the cave through the hole.

"Hold on tightly", she shouted to her friends, "we're going through".

She eased her long body through the gap, out into the open loch, and headed towards the surface, with the mermaids clinging to her tail. They surfaced, took in air, then Nessie took Jess and Tilly home.

She made sure the girls were safe before she herself headed home for her supper. As she swam away she could hear Tilly and Jess shouting after her...

"Thank you Nessie - we love you"..

She didn't know what happened back there and during supper she wanted to ask her mum about the thing she was able to do with her eyes, but she could hear mum saying. "Och, don't be silly Nessie" ... so she ate her supper in silence.

"Are you all right, Nessie? You're awfy quiet tonight - I hope you hivnae been up to more mischief".

"I'm fine mum - just a bit tired".

After tea she curled herself around her favourite rock and sighed contentedly. Tomorrow was Sunday. Nessie, wondering what it would bring, gave a big yawn and fell fast asleep.

Puffy the Puffer Fish

PUFFY - THE PUFFER FISH

Nessie was barely awake one morning when her mermaid friends - Jess and Tilly - came swimming into her cave, their long blonde hair floating all around them.

"Puffy needs help - Puffy needs help — come quickly, Nessie".

Puffy was another friend — a huge prickly puffer fish — normally long and slim, but if danger approaches, his body blows up into a big ball, which is covered in poisonous spikes. Normally Puffy can control himself but, lately, he had been having accidents.

"He can't stop blowing up", said Tilly, "he's already poisoned five jellyfish by mistake. We have to help him".

Nessie, Tilly and Jess swam towards Puffy's cave and when they went inside, Puffy was sitting - all blown up, crying.

"I don't know what to do — please don't come near me or I will poison you — but I don't mean to" he said, with a sad look in his eyes.

"Don't worry", said Nessie, "we're here to help you". Tilly and Jess shared a boulder while Nessie coiled herself around an even bigger one.

"Now, let me think", said Nessie… "I've got it — what about trying to relax your mind? We'll all do it together. Everyone - close your eyes and breathe in through your nose slowly, then breathe out through your mouth. Repeat… a few times more", she said. When they opened their eyes and looked at Puffy, his body had shrunk and he was back down to his normal, thin self.

"See," said Nessie. "It works".

"Oh thank you", said Puffy and they all swam out of the cave and headed for the play area.

The play area consisted of swings and various tunnels in which the loch creatures loved to play.

Puffy swam into one of the tunnels but, unbeknown to him, a huge red crab had entered the other end and was swimming sideways towards him.

"Get out of my way", shouted the crab, "or I'll nip you with my pincers".

Puffy felt a threatening feeling coming on and couldn't control himself. He puffed up, then puffed up more - until he filled the tunnel. Luckily the crab had a hard shell and couldn't be poisoned, but he did get stuck. Puffy was blocking his way and he couldn't turn round, so they both started yelling...

"Help...help"...

Nessie, with her extra sensory hearing, heard the cries and headed for the tunnel. She looked in one end and saw Puffy's ball-shaped body wedged from wall to wall.

"Listen to me, Puffy" she shouted. "Close your eyes and breathe in slowly through your nose, then breathe out slowly through your mouth".

Puffy did what he was told and slowly he began to shrink. What he didn't see was Nessie staring at his back with her special eyes. Yellow rays blazed into Puffy's back and, slowly but surely, his big fat body began to get smaller... and smaller...
When Puffy was normal size again he turned round and swam free of the tunnel. The crab grumpily followed him.

"About time", the crab said, as it scuttled off sideways.

Back at Puffy's cave, Nessie said. "Puffy, I think we need to do some more work on your deep breathing" — and they all laughed. When Nessie got home, her mum was waiting for her.

"Settle yourself down", she said; "I have something to tell you. You never knew your father, Nessie, but it's time I told you something about him. He began working with the Royal Navy during the war. His job was to swim far out to sea, seeking German submarines. Your father had special powers, Nessie, which were passed down to him by his own father.

He had this amazing ability of melting objects with his eyes. He would stare — and stare — and a beam of bright light came out of his eyes and was able to destroy whatever he stared at".

"I can do that, Mum," Nessie said.

"I wondered if it had been passed to you" his Mum said. "Tell me what's been happening to you, lass".

Nessie told her Mum the things she had been doing with Tilly and Jess. Her Mum sat quietly, listening and nodding.

"You have your father's gift Nessie, but you must use it carefully and only for the good of others — do you understand?"

"Yes, I think so Mum", and Nessie yawned .
"Get some sleep now, lass" her Mum said.

While Nessie curled herself around her favourite rock her Mum grew worried. She hadn't told Nessie what happened to her father. She didn't tell her that he was blown up by a German torpedo and died instantly.

He was a hero, according to the Navy, but he was also a well kept secret. She still missed him, but hoped dearly that Nessie would use her power well. If bad people got wind of Nessie's power, her mum knew they would hunt her and try to capture her.

She must be watchful and protect her daughter…

NESSIE'S ADVENTURES - No. 4
The Urquhart Castle incident...

The Urquhart Castle Incident....

Nessie awoke suddenly. She felt trembling beneath her and heard a noise in the distance. At first she thought she was dreaming, but the noise continued. She swam out of the cave and up to the surface of the water. It was still dark but in the distance she saw bright lights. Urquhart Castle stood on the edge of the loch and as she swam towards it she realised the brightness wasn't lights — it was fire…! Urquhart Castle was one of Scotland's biggest castles and was home to Robert the Bruce in the fourteenth century. Now in ruins, but still towering over the loch, it remains a popular visitor attraction. But - right now - the trees and shrubs which surrounded the castle were on fire.

Nessie doubled back and headed towards the ranger station, which sat on the bank of the loch a mile from the castle. She circled around outside it, making her unusual whooping sound, but there was no response. She then opened her big eyes wide, stuck out her long neck, and stared at the ranger's window. Her bright yellow beam lit up the whole room inside, awakening Roger, the duty ranger. He looked out of his window and saw Nessie frantically splashing around in the water. He knew Nessie, so realised immediately there must be something wrong. He quickly dressed and jumped into his speedboat.

"Lead on, Nessie" he shouted.

When they came upon the fire, the ranger radioed the local fire brigade, who arrived within ten minutes. Anxiously, he watched the firemen begin putting out the fire. Meanwhile Nessie swam round the edge of the loch until she came upon a small boat, which had been docked at an old jetty. She saw two boys sitting in the boat and swam very slowly and silently just beneath the water - until she was close

enough to hear laughter. The boys were discussing what they had just done.

"That was a good idea Jack, bringing the can of petrol", the first one said.

"Did you see how quickly the fire started when we threw the petrol bombs? Wow - it took my breath away."

The boys, never thinking for a moment how a fire could spread among dry shrubs, laughed with wide eyes, re-living the scene, each taking a slug of whisky and passing the bottle.

Quietly, using her small needle-like teeth, Nessie bit through the thin rope which held the boat to the jetty and, unable to be seen in the dark, she positioned her broad back underneath the small speedboat. Slowly, and very quietly, she weaved her body through the water, taking the boat with her. The boys were so busy talking and swigging the whisky, it took a while before they realised they were moving away from the jetty.

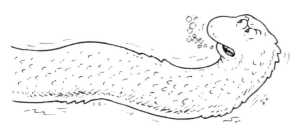

"Hey..... what's happening?" one of them shouted; "the boat — it's moving".

"How can it move without the engine?" the other boy said and then, through the darkness, the burning bushes in front of the castle came into view. The firemen were still frantically hosing the area while, in the still-smouldering flames, the ranger's boat with its searchlight sat patiently in the water. "Look" said one of the boys — "the ranger!"...
But there was nothing the boys could do. They couldn't jump into the water as it was too dark and deep. Neither could they start their engine, because it was sitting too high out of the water. They sat in their boat - motionless - helplessly drifting towards the side of the ranger's boat. They were clueless, of course, as to how THEIR boat was moving without the engine!

"Ah, the culprits", said the ranger, as the boys' boat nudged alongside his own one. He thought the boys looked very young, was sure that their parents had NO idea where they were and what they were drinking....but they were about to find out.

"We'll go on a little trip, shall we, boys?"

The ranger tied the boys' boat to his own and helped them climb into it. Nessie slowly slipped under the water. The boys were towed back round the loch to the ranger station, where two policemen were waiting. They would handle things from now on.

"Thank you, Nessie" the ranger shouted into the darkness. The boys peered across the loch into the eerie blackness... looking around to see who or where Nessie was.. .but, of course, she was nowhere to be seen...

Nessie returned home and went straight to her favourite rock, where she contentedly curled herself around it and, almost immediately, drifted off into a deep sleep.

Goodbye to Mum... And Enter - The Navy...

The gathering was small, both under the water and above it. Nessie's mother had passed away peacefully and Nessie was surrounded by all her friends. It was customary that when a loch creature died, it supplied nourishment to all creature friends who lived nearby.

Nessie's mum's body was cast adrift into the deepest part of the loch and was never seen again. Nessie swam to the surface, where Roger Ranger sat in his boat along with his assistant Bill Ranger. They had known Nessie's mother for a long time and came to pay their respects.

They sat with heads bowed and, when Nessie appeared on the surface of the water, both Rangers gave her a salute. She nodded her head up and down before disappearing back down - into the depths of the loch.

All Nessie's friends were gathered in her cave. Jess and Tilly, the twin mermaids, cooked delicious pots of scrumptious snails and jellied eels.

Puffy the puffer fish sang songs, Terry Trout clapped his fins together and even Squiddy the giant squid, whom they had now befriended, sat on a rock and waved all of his eight legs in time to Puffy's singing.

The party ended at midnight. Although she missed her mum, Nessie was now an adult and had to force herself to get on with life.

Nessie enjoyed swimming around the loch, doing her usual three—hump routine, showing off to the tourists, especially when the sun was shining. One morning, she saw Roger Ranger driving his speedboat very fast towards her. He waved to Nessie, then waved her over. He stopped his boat alongside her and took a seat. Looking over the side of the boat, with a frown on his face, he began speaking quietly to Nessie.

"I was a young ranger when your father was alive, Nessie. I don't know how much your mother has told you about him but he was a very brave monster. He saved hundreds of people from drowning over the years before he was taken from the loch. A Navy boat had arrived in the loch one day, looking for your father. They used stun rifles to fire bullets into his body, which made him sleepy. Divers then tied ropes around him and the boat sailed away — dragging your father behind it".

"But why was he taken away?" Nessie asked, her huge eyes staring up at her favourite ranger. "I heard later he was put to work by the Royal Navy,"

Roger replied. "They trained him to look for enemy submarines during the war".

"What's a submarine?" Nessie asked.

"It's like a ship but travels under the water" Roger Ranger explained. "It carries people and torpedoes which, when fired, can blow up other submarines or ships. Your father was very good at his job, Nessie, but the German Government also found out about his special powers".

"Is that the same special powers which I have?" Nessie asked.

"Yes, and our Government kept those special powers a secret from everyone, just like your mum and I are doing here. We don't want you ever to be taken away from us".

"What happened to my father? How did he die?"

"I'm afraid the secret got out, Nessie, and — one dark night — the enemy was waiting for him. They fired a torpedo and it didn't miss. I'm sorry Nessie, but you see why we can't let people know about you, so you must be very careful about how you use your powers".

"I will," said Nessie, as she swam off.

Roger Ranger watched her swim around the loch, looking for people to rescue. There was always somebody needing help, whether it be a boat in trouble or a child swimming too far from the shore. What Roger Ranger didn't tell Nessie was that he had heard a rumour that the Navy would be sending people soon, to seek out Nessie. He always wondered how word got out about Nessie and her father. He began to suspect there must be a spy in the camp.

Then the day came...

Roger Ranger looked out of his window one afternoon and caught sight of a large speedboat, with RN painted in big letters on the side. He followed it with his binoculars. He could see three men dressed in frogmen's gear, one man looking over the side, and one man driving the boat.

The men were seated, looking at some sort of screen. The man looking over the side was handling a piece of equipment. Roger Ranger had heard of a gadget which, using ultrasound, could find sea creatures. The gadget hanging in the water picked up signals and flashed images on to a screen. 'They are looking for Nessie' Roger Ranger thought to himself. Then he spotted four underwater rifles. He must do something...

The boat in question had arrived in the late afternoon, so there wasn't much daylight left. Roger Ranger waited until the men finally packed up and left. He suspected they didn't realise just how deep the loch was and how long the job would take. But he knew they would be back in the morning. He jumped into his boat and headed out to the middle of the loch. He too had a piece of equipment, which he began to dangle over the side of his boat.

This was to signal Nessie; in no time at all, she raised her head above the water - just a few feet from Roger Ranger.

"Nessie, remember what I told you about your father?" She immediately nodded. "There were men in a boat on the loch earlier today. I think they were looking for you, Nessie. You must stop doing your displays on top of the water - just for a while - until the men go away". He also told her about the ultrasound equipment they had and how easily they could track her down. "You know the places to hide, Nessie, so tell your friends to keep hidden too". Nessie nodded….then submerged.

Roger Ranger returned to his station to find his assistant, Bill Ranger, speaking on the telephone.

He heard him say,

"That's too bad you couldn't find her……… okay, I'll see you tomorrow".

"Who was that?" Roger asked Bill.

"Oh, nobody — I'll be off then — see you in the morning".

When he had gone, Roger lifted the phone and pressed its 'last number redial' button. The voice on the other end answered "Special Operations". NOW Roger knew who the spy was...

The next morning, Nessie did exactly what Roger Ranger had told her. She swam around, keeping underwater, and told her friends to keep away from the surface. When she told them why, their offer of support was instant. "We'll help you", said Jess and Tilly.

"Me too", said Puffy.
"And me," said Terry Trout.

Later on, Jess and Tilly came swimming into Nessie's cave . They shouted, "It's the big boat you told us about — it's up there", said Tilly. "It's up there", said Jess. The twins were looking VERY frightened.

"Go back to your cave and stay there" Nessie said. "Don't worry girls, it will go away when it gets dark". But Nessie was wrong. The Navy boat had huge spotlamps, which lit up the water after the sun had set. The divers jumped into the water after the ultrasonic machine had shown a shadow on the screen, but they could only go down so far. They didn't realise just how deep the loch was. Nessie and her friends watched them from a distance and, when the divers got too close to Nessie, Jess and Tilly would swim between the men to put them off the scent. After a while the men gave up and left the loch, only to return again the next day.

Roger Ranger drew up beside the Navy boat next morning and tried to warn the men that some of the creatures in the loch could be very dangerous. He knew men who had dived deep down into the loch in the past - and were never seen again.

"We have our orders, sir," one of the men said, "and I'm afraid we can't leave until we find your Nessie. Perhaps you could help us? You know the loch well and are probably aware of Nessie's hiding places. If you could show us where to look, we would appreciate it".

"I can't do that. My job is to help preserve the area and all creatures within the loch", Roger replied, firmly.

"I can't force you, sir but, if you won't help, then we may have to use explosive materials to help us flush out the monster".

"You can't do that — this whole area is protected". These being Roger Ranger's last words, he sped off back to his station to make some calls. His first call was directly to the Scottish Government and he demanded to speak to someone in authority. There was nobody available to speak to him. His second call was to the Westminster Government, where he managed to speak with someone who was willing to help him. Meanwhile, the divers continued to dive - and prepare their explosives.

Nessie swam out of her cave to stretch her body. She had been cooped up for too long. She began swimming upwards but, on seeing two figures ahead of her, she slowed to a halt.

The frogmen were placing something silvery - coloured between two rocks. One frogman signalled to the other, holding up five fingers on one hand. Then they both swam to the surface. Nessie stayed still, not understanding what was going on. All of a sudden a huge shadow passed over her... it was heading towards the silver object.

It was Squiddy, the giant squid! He settled himself down, covering the object with his large body and winding his eight tentacles around and around until he looked like a giant ball. A minute later Nessie felt her body shudder, ripples surrounded her... then all was still.

She swam back down to her cave and Squiddy followed.

"What was that?" she asked Squiddy and, as she cast her eyes over Squiddy's huge body, she noticed that two of his tentacles were missing. "Squiddy — you've lost two of your legs — are you in pain?"

"That was an explosive device I sat on. I couldn't let it hurt you, Nessie but no, I'm not in pain. Besides, I have six other legs - so I'll be alright" he said, bravely.

Nessie burst into tears. "Oh, Squiddy, you are a true friend".

The next morning, Nessie and Squiddy swam around in the deepest part of the loch. They knew they would be safe there. They swam in and out of the long thick reeds which were attached to the floor of the loch. Squiddy swam ahead of Nessie, but she didn't notice that he had suddenly stopped, because she went crashing into the back of him.

"Look!" said Squiddy, "frogmen ahead".

Nessie peered into the reeds until she saw three figures, with what looked like guns in their hands. Only, they weren't swimming — they were flaying around in the water, looking as if they were being strangled by the reeds.

"They are too deep" said Squiddy — "they've dived too deep. Men can't survive down here".
"I have to help them" said Nessie. "After all, that's what I do".

"All right" said Squiddy. "I'll help too, but we have to be careful — they have guns".

As they swam nearer, they saw that the men were really in trouble. The reeds had wrapped themselves around their bodies, stopping them from surfacing. Soon they would run out of air and drown.

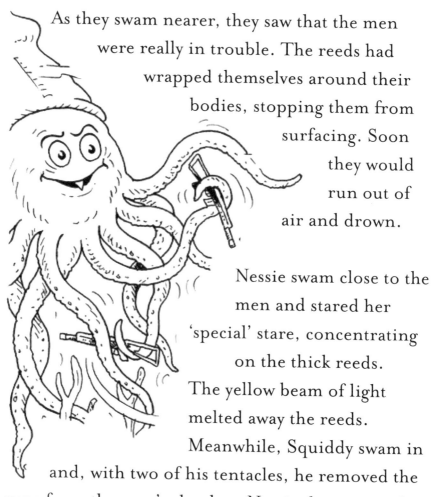

Nessie swam close to the men and stared her 'special' stare, concentrating on the thick reeds. The yellow beam of light melted away the reeds. Meanwhile, Squiddy swam in and, with two of his tentacles, he removed the guns from the men's clutches. Nessie then opened her large jaws, scooped up one man after the other and swam to the surface.

She raised herself high out of the water and placed the frogmen, gently, inside the boat, then disappeared under the water again.

The other two men on the boat couldn't believe their eyes. A monster? With THREE men in its huge mouth? The two men grabbed rifles and began firing into the water.

"Stop... stop," one of the frogmen said weakly. "The monster saved us — it actually SAVED us!". The two men stopped firing and concentrated on helping the frogmen. They started the engine and pointed the boat towards the ranger station.

Luckily Roger Ranger was there and, when he saw the condition of the men, he rang for an ambulance, then helped carry the men into his warm office.

"What happened?" Roger asked. The men were keen to tell him about the monster. "Ah — that would be the very monster I believe you were looking for" Roger said. That was Nessie, who spends her time saving lives, here in the loch".

One of the men said, "I think the guys will be alright but what just happened was unbelievable. If it hadn't been for Nessie, our men would have drowned".

The ambulance arrived and took away the three men for a check-up at the local hospital, while the other two boarded their motor boat, offered their thanks, then said their farewells to Roger Ranger.

The Navy boat NEVER returned. A few weeks later, Roger Ranger received a letter from the Government, thanking him for his help and informing him that Nessie would be free to live the rest of her life in peace. He received another letter informing him he would have a new assistant by the end of the month.

Roger Ranger jumped into his boat and sped out to the middle of the loch, where he sat and waited. Within five minutes, Nessie appeared beside his boat and he told her about the letter.

She nodded her head three times then happily disappeared into the depths of the loch...

Nessie couldn't wait to tell her friends the good news...

NESSIE'S ADVENTURES-No. 5
Goodbye to Mum...
and Enter the Navy...